Wake-Up Kisses   Text copyright © 2002 by Pamela Duncan Edwards   Illustrations copyright © 2002 by Henry Cole
Printed in the U.S.A. All rights reserved.   www.harperchildrens.com

Library of Congress Cataloging-in-Publication Data
Edwards, Pamela Duncan.
Wake-up kisses / Pamela Duncan Edwards ; [illustrated by] Henry Cole.—1st ed.
p.   cm.
Summary: Katydids, owls, opossums, and other nocturnal animal mothers and babies wake up to a bright moon
and a night to be filled with activities.
ISBN 0-06-623976-1 — ISBN 0-06-623977-X (lib. bdg.)
[1. Nocturnal animals—Fiction. 2. Night—Fiction. 3. Animals—Infancy—Fiction. 4. Stories in rhyme.]
I. Cole, Henry, 1955– ill. II. Title.
PZ8.3.E283 Wak 2002
[E]—dc21   2001024395
                                                                                                                                         CIP
                                                                                                                                          AC
Typography by Robbin Gourley   1 2 3 4 5 6 7 8 9 10 ❖ First Edition

Wake-Up Kisses

By Pamela Duncan Edwards ❖ Illustrated by Henry Cole

HarperCollins Publishers

The sun has gone, the moon is bright,
The air is filled with sounds of night.

"Katydid! Katydid!" Katydid's calling.
"Everyone up! The dark is falling."

"Wake up!" hoots Owl. "T'wit, t'woo!
Open your eyes! There's lots to do."

"Rise and shine!" Field Mouse squeaks,
Stuffing breakfast in babies' cheeks.

"Lazyheads!" Opossum hisses.
"I'm waiting to get my wake-up kisses."

Cries Mother Bat, "It's time to fly,
Gliding-flapping through the sky."

"Stretch those wings! Chitter! Chitter!"
Cries Flying Squirrel to her litter.

"Croak! Croak!" Tree Frog sings.
"Let's get busy doing things!"

In overcoats striped white and black,
Little skunks wait for their twilight snack.

Growls Raccoon, "I've made plans!
I'll teach you to raid the garbage cans."

They're waking up, our nighttime friends.
Their day begins as our day ends.
We're snuggled in bed. Time to turn out the light,
But we'll see them in our dreams tonight.

For Hannah and Maddy,
my sweet little friends,
with love, P.D.E.

To Laura,
with love, H.C.